SUN & MOON
MEMOIR

Legends in the Making

KATIE MONOHAN

THIS MEMOIR BELONGS TO:

_____

In ancient whispers, it's said that Sun and Moon were separated by jealous schemes yet found their way back to each other in the magic of the celestial sky.

Cosmic tales recount Sun sending Moon golden gifts of warmth, each ray a token of undying affection; their cosmic embrace is felt in every sunrise.

Moon chases Sun in a dance across the sky, a love story painted in every sunrise and sunset.

Moonbeams are Moon's whispers of love to Sun, lighting the night with tender affection.

Sun and Moon's embrace during eclipses reveals their timeless passion, uniting in a cosmic kiss.

Each eclipse is a moment of cosmic union, with Sun and Moon locked in the embrace of everlasting love.

Stars are remnants of Sun and Moon's first celestial kisses scattered across the night sky.

Sun and Moon's playful pursuit across the skies, laughter echoing in twilight's veil, a cosmic game revealing the joy of celestial bonds.

Clouds are veils that separate Sun and Moon, yet their love shines through even when the fog shrouds them completely, enduring the temporary separation.

Celestial bodies are love notes exchanged between Sun and Moon, orbits and phases, a dance of eternal affection.

In the celestial ballet, Sun and Moon waltz, each a partner in the other's eternal embrace.

Solar flares are Sun's bursts of affection, reaching out across the cosmos to touch Moon's heart.

A lunar rainbow is a display of Moon's love, arcs of color dancing in the night sky.

Shooting stars are whispered promises of forever exchanged between Sun and Moon, streaks of devotion across the heavens.

Solar eclipses are Sun's tender kisses upon Moon's face, a moment of celestial intimacy.

Lunar eclipses are Moon's embrace of Sun's fiery passion, a dance of light and shadow.

Comet trails are paths Sun and Moon trace across the sky, marking celestial rendezvous.

Aurora borealis is Sun and Moon's symphony of light, painting polar skies with luminous love.

Through solar winds, Sun's whispers of love reach Moon, a message of eternal longing and devotion.

Lunar phases are Moon's expressions of longing for Sun, each cycle a verse in their timeless love song.

Constellations are storytellers of Sun and Moon's epic romance, etching their tale in stars.

Solar storms are Sun's tempestuous declarations of passion, lighting up the sky in bursts of ardor.

Lunar halos are Moon's
radiant crowns, symbolizing
regal love for Sun.

Nebulae are celestial tapestries woven by Sun and Moon, threads of light intertwining in cosmic artistry.

Solar rainbows are Sun's colorful displays of affection, arcs of light bridging the celestial expanse.

Lunar mists are Moon's veiled caresses, soft touches across the night sky.

Stellar nurseries are cradles of new stars born from Sun and Moon's eternal embrace, a testament to their undying passion.

The solar corona is Sun's luminous aura, a halo of love encircling Moon in a cosmic dance.

Shooting stars are Sun and Moon's
celestial whispers, streaks of luminescence
carrying their messages of love.

Solar winds are Sun's gentle caresses upon Moon's face, whispers of warmth across the night sky.

Twilight is the time when Sun and Moon share loving secrets, painting the sky in hues of whispered confessions.

Rainbows are Sun's gifts to
Moon, arches of color painted across
the heavens to celebrate their love.

Dusk and dawn are meeting points for
Sun and Moon, where they exchange
tender kisses across the horizon.

Sun's warmth is a caress to
Moon's cool surface, a gentle
touch across the cosmos.

Sun's rays are love's tendrils, reaching out to embrace Moon each day.

Celestial whispers carry the legend of forbidden love between Sun and Moon, their cosmic union giving birth to Earth in a symphony of passion and creation.

Cloudless nights are the stage for Sun and Moon's unobstructed love, their brilliance illuminating the darkness.

Stars sing ballads of Sun and Moon's eternal romance, melody woven into the fabric of the universe.

Sunsets are promises from Moon to Sun, a vow to guide her through the night's embrace.

Whispered in starlight is the tale of Sun and Moon granting wishes where their radiant paths converge, showering seekers with dreams fulfilled and love's celestial blessings.

Mythic verses praise Sun's gift of fire and
passion, kindling mortals' hearts with ardor and
empathy, igniting souls with love's eternal spark.

Tales speak of Sun and Moon as star-crossed lovers, separated by the vastness of the sky yet eternally bound by luminous affection, their story woven in threads of stardust.

An epic saga sings of Sun and Moon, whose radiant union during eclipses symbolizes perfect harmony. Their embrace echoed through the ages in soft whispers.

Folklore weaves a tale of Sun's fiery passion igniting Moon's extraordinary grace, painting the skies with colors of romance, their love mirrored in every twilight.

A romantic saga hails Sun and Moon as soulmates, destined in an eternal chase across the heavens, their devotion echoing every dawn and dusk.

Ancient legends revere Moon's gentle guidance—
lighting the way for Sun's fiery passions to bloom in
the hearts of mortals, a celestial dance of inspiration.

Enchanting myths reveal Sun and Moon's secret meetings at dusk, whispers of love in hues of color, painting the sky with twilight's embrace.

Moon's phases reflect his longing for Sun, waxing and waning with the rhythm of their eternal bond.

The morning dew is Moon's tears of sorrow as he bids farewell to his beloved Sun each day.

Sun and Moon race across the heavens to protect Earth, leading to endless cycles of day and night.

Elders speak of a prophetic legend in which Sun and Moon unite in an eclipse, marking a time of wondrous change.

Whispers of old legends tell of Moon's benevolence—gifting mortals with wind and valor and bestowing upon them endless protection.

Timeless legends revere Sun and Moon as Earth's guardians, ensuring her eternal dance, harmonizing light and shadow to bestow balance upon the world.

An enduring myth unveils Sun and Moon's respite in a hidden garden. Their mingled light birthing the most exquisite blooms, a testament to love's enduring grace.

A legend of Sun and Moon's eternal love, their celestial dance across the heavens, is a testament to timeless romance, whispered in every constellation.

Legends speak of Sun and Moon as celestial lovers, their gentle gazes igniting the night sky in cosmic passion's dance, a symphony of celestial love.

Mythic lore speaks of Sun and Moon exchanging tender kisses across the horizon, their eternal embrace casting a radiant glow upon the world, an eternal flame.

Songs echo of Moon serenading Sun with silver streaks of light, whispering love notes that caress the night, a melody of cosmic adoration.

Legends murmur of Moon's shimmering tears, reflecting Sun's longing gaze as they yearn across the celestial expanse, their love story written in the night's tapestry.

Celestial ballads sing of Sun and Moon's
tender caresses, their light intertwining in a
luminous embrace, a dance of eternal devotion.

Romantic legends etch Sun and Moon's whispered promises in constellations across the night sky, every star a testament to their undying bond.

Timeless tales speak of Sun and Moon's enduring love, their radiant bond a beacon of hope and romance for all who gaze upon the heavens, their love story etched in eternity's canvas.

Celestial whispers speak of Sun and Moon's eternal courtship, their dance across the sky a symphony of undying love.

Sunsets mark the moment when Sun and Moon exchange tender gazes across the horizon, a silent promise of eternal devotion.

Dawn breaks as Moon bids farewell to Sun, their parting kiss painting the sky in hues of longing and anticipation.

Shooting stars are whispers of love
exchanged between Sun and Moon,
each trail a testament to their eternal bond.

Solar eclipses are moments of divine embrace,
Sun and Moon locked in a passionate union
visible to all who gaze skyward.

Lunar phases reflect the ebb and flow of Sun and Moon's affection, waxing and waning in harmony with their eternal love.

In an ancient tale, Sun follows Moon to Milky Way, drawn by his declaration of love after the deception that once drove them apart.

After coalescing their hearts for all eternity, Sun and Moon sacrificed their celestial forms and descended to Earth, embracing mortal lives to protect their daughter as her devoted guardians.

Made in the USA
Columbia, SC
20 June 2024

37015587R00083